The NEW BEAR at SCHOOL

For Dr. Elizabeth Marsden — always a smile. — C.W.

For the amazing Early Years Team at Piddle Valley. Thanks for everything! — T.W.

Text copyright © 2007 by Carrie Weston
Illustrations copyright © 2007 by Tim Warnes

Library of Congress Cataloging-in-Publication Data
is available upon request.

ISBN-13: 978-0-545-05783-7
ISBN-10: 0-545-05783-3

10 9 8 7 6 5 4 3 2 1   08 09 10 11 12
Printed in China
The text type was set in Extreme

First American edition, July 2008

*With thanks to Michael Bond and HarperCollins for their kind permission
in allowing Paddington Bear to make three and a bit appearances in this book.*

Carrie Weston • Tim Warnes
The NEW BEAR at SCHOOL

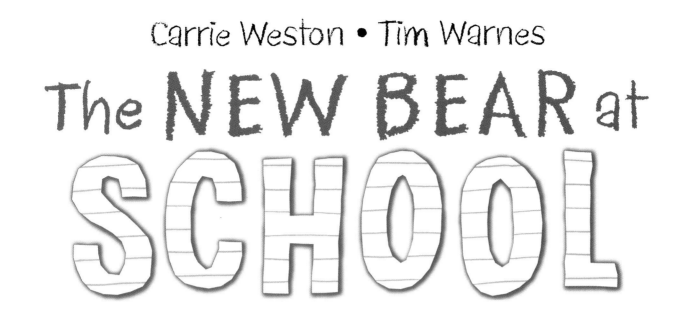

Scholastic Press • New York

0 1 2 3 4 5 6 7 8 9 10
zero one two three four five six seven eight nine ten

The day that Miss Cluck said
there was going to be a new
animal in the class, everyone
was very excited.

Monday

Wednesday

Thursday

day

1p

2p

milk 5p

Tuesday— BORIS!

REGISTER

music box ♫

When Miss Cluck said that
the new animal was a **bear**,
the other animals squealed
with delight.

Leticia the rabbit wondered if it might be a fluffy pink bear, like the one on her lunch box.

Maxwell the mole wanted a floppy brown bear with velvet paws.

The mice hoped for a bear in Wellingtons and a blue coat.

Fergus the fox cub thought any teddy bear would be just fine.

So, when the classroom
door opened

and Miss Cluck
introduced Boris,

everyone . . .

screamed!

For Boris wasn't a teddy bear.

He was an enormous, hairy, scary grizzly bear!

Miss Cluck told Boris she'd give him his uniform tomorrow, and found him a seat next to Maxwell.

But as he sat down, there was a loud **crack.**

It made Maxwell hide his face in his paws.

"Oh, Boris!" said Miss Cluck. "Why don't you sit on the floor instead?"

Miss Cluck gave Boris
a new book and a pencil.
He was very
proud indeed.

With a big, friendly grin, Boris turned to show the mice.

But Boris
forgot how
fierce
his teeth
were.

He forgot how
big
his paws
were.

And he forgot how **sharp** his claws were.

Somehow, the mice got scattered across the classroom.
Somehow, the pages of his new book got ripped.

Somehow, | there | was | panic | everywhere.

"Boris is too **big!**" cried one little mouse.

"Boris is too **hairy!**" yelled another.

"Boris is too **scary!**"
they all squeaked together.

"**Oh, Boris!**" said Miss Cluck. "Please try to be more careful."

At lunchtime everyone sat together.

There was not enough room on the bench
for Boris, but nobody moved over.

So he sat all by himself and dipped his big paw into the large jar of honey his mommy had packed for him.

When lunchtime was over Miss Cluck said everyone could go off and play.

The mice began a game
of hide-and-seek.

"1 . . . 2 . . . 3 . . ."

Everyone ran
to find a place
to hide.
But Boris
was too
big.

So Boris shut his eyes and counted instead.

"One . . . two . . . three . . .
coming to get you,"

Boris boomed.

"Eeek!"

"Stop!
Stop!"

"No!
No!"

Maxwell ran
crying to
Miss Cluck.

?

"Let's go inside and play some quiet games," said Miss Cluck, "and Boris, **please** try to be less scary, dear."

red orange
blue purple
yellow green

The animals sat together in a circle.

There was no space for Boris.

Boris had nobody to play with and nobody to talk to.
Tears filled his big, brown eyes, rolled down
his long nose, and splashed to the floor.

"I'm a
scary bear,"
he sniffed.

"I'm a
hairy bear,"
he sobbed.

"I'm just a great
big
grizzly bear."

It seemed like a very long afternoon.

At last it was time
to go home.

Miss Cluck stood and waved as the
animals set off through the woods.

Leticia hopped
along the bank.

Fergus chased
the little mice
around a tree.

Maxwell scampered
through the leaves.

Boris plodded along far behind.

Suddenly, from a hollow tree leapt . . .

the
rat
pack!

"Well, well, if it isn't the **crybabies**," said the meanest rat.

poke!

"Help!"

Leticia, Maxwell, Fergus, and the mice trembled while the rat pack circled around them.

The rats didn't see Boris
plodding along the path.

All Boris could see was lots
of excitement ahead.

He wanted to join the fun.

Boris stood up tall to greet
the new friends with
his **biggest,** widest
bear grin and . . .

"Quick! Run! It's a hairy, scary grizzly bear!"

The rotten rats ran away as fast as their skinny legs could carry them.

"But I only wanted to say hello . . . ." called Boris.

When Boris turned around,
the other animals cheered.

"Boris is a hairy bear," they sang.

"Boris is a scary bear," they chanted.

"We're so glad that
Boris is our grizzly bear!"

Suddenly, Boris felt very shy.
"If you're going to be a bear,"
he said very gently,
"then it's probably best to be a
hairy, scary grizzly bear."

The next day at school, the animals couldn't wait
to tell Miss Cluck how Boris had saved them from
the nasty rat pack.

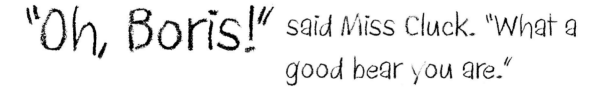

"Oh, Boris!" said Miss Cluck. "What a
good bear you are."

At story time everyone rushed to gather around Miss Cluck. There wasn't much room once Boris had sat down.

But the rest of the class didn't mind one little bit...

. . . they all had a soft,
warm place to sit, after all!